YEARLING BOOKS

Since 1966, Yearling has been the

leading name in classic and award-winning

literature for young readers.

With a wide variety of titles,

Yearling paperbacks entertain, inspire,

and encourage a love of reading.

VISIT

RANDOMHOUSE.COM/KIDS

**TO FIND THE PERFECT BOOK, PLAY GAMES,
AND MEET FAVORITE AUTHORS!**

The One in the Middle Is the Green Kangaroo

Judy Blume

The One in the Middle Is the Green Kangaroo

Illustrated by Amy Aitken

A YEARLING BOOK

Published by Yearling, an imprint of Random House Children's Books
a division of Random House, Inc., New York

Visit us on the Web! www.randomhouse.com/kids

Educators and librarians, for a variety of teaching tools, visit us at
www.randomhouse.com/teachers

ISBN: 0-440-46731-4

Reprinted by arrangement with Simon & Schuster Books for Young Readers

Printed in the United States of America

November 1986

80 79 78 77 76 75

OPM

For Randy and Larry,
who have been there from the beginning

The One in the Middle Is the Green Kangaroo

Freddy Dissel had two problems. One was his older brother Mike. The other was his younger sister Ellen. Freddy thought a lot about being the one in the middle. But there was nothing he could do about it. He felt like the peanut butter part of a sandwich, squeezed between Mike and Ellen.

Every year Mike got new clothes. He grew too big for his old ones. But Mike's old clothes weren't too small for Freddy. They fit him just fine.

Freddy used to have a room of his own. That was before Ellen was born. Now Ellen had a room of *her* own. Freddy moved in with Mike. Mom and Dad said, "It's the boys' room." But they couldn't fool Freddy. He knew better!

Once Freddy tried to join Mike and
his friends. But Mike said, "Get out of the
way, kid!" So Freddy tried to play with Ellen. Ellen didn't understand how to play
his way. She messed up all of Freddy's
things. Freddy got mad and pinched her.
Ellen screamed.

"Freddy Dissel!" Mom yelled. "You shouldn't be mean to Ellen. She's smaller than you. She's just a baby!"

Ellen didn't look like a baby to Freddy. She didn't sound like a baby either. She even goes to nursery school, Freddy thought. *Some baby!*

Freddy figured things would never get better for him. He would always be a great big middle nothing!

Then one day Freddy heard about the school play. Mike had never been in a play. Ellen had never been in a play. This was his chance to do something special. Freddy decided he would try it.

He waited two whole days before he went to his teacher. "Ms. Gumber," he said. "I want to be in the school play."

Qq Rr Ss Tt Uu Vv Ww

Ms. Gumber smiled and shook her head. "I'm sorry, Freddy," she said. "The play is being done by the fifth and sixth graders. The big boys and girls, like Mike."

Freddy looked at the floor and mumbled. "That figures!" He started to walk away.

"Wait a minute, Freddy," Ms. Gumber called. "I'll talk to Ms. Matson anyway. She's in charge of the play. I'll find out if they need any second graders to help."

Finally, Ms. Gumber told Freddy that Ms. Matson needed someone to play a special part. Ms. Gumber said, "Go to the auditorium this afternoon. Maybe you'll get the part."

"Great!" Freddy hollered.

Later he went to the auditorium. Ms. Matson was waiting for him. Freddy walked right up close to her. He said, "I want to be in the play."

Ms. Matson asked him to go up on the stage and say that again – in a very loud voice.

Freddy had never been on the stage. It was big. It made him feel small. He looked out at Ms. Matson.

"I AM FREDDY," he shouted. "I WANT TO BE IN THE PLAY."

"Good," Ms. Matson called. "Now then Freddy, can you jump?"

What kind of question was that, Freddy wondered. Of course he could jump. He was in second grade, wasn't he? So he jumped. He jumped all around the stage — big jumps and little jumps. When he was through Ms. Matson clapped her hands, and Freddy climbed down from the stage.

"I think you will be fine as the Green Kangaroo, Freddy," Ms. Matson said. "It's a very important part."

Freddy didn't tell anyone at home about the play until dinner time. Then he said, "Guess what, everyone? Guess what I'm going to be?"

No one paid any attention to what Freddy was saying. They were too busy eating.

"I'm going to be in a play," Freddy said. "I'm going to be the Green Kangaroo!"

Mike choked on his potato and knocked over a whole glass of milk. Ellen laughed because Mike spilled his milk. Dad jumped up. He patted Mike on the back to make him stop choking.

Mom ran to get the sponge. She cleaned up the spilled milk. Freddy just sat there and smiled.

"What did you say?" Mike asked.

"I *said* I'm going to be in the school play. I *said* I'm going to be the Green Kangaroo!"

"It can't be true," Mike yelled. "Why would they pick you?"

"Because I can jump," Freddy said.

"I can jump, too," Ellen said.

"*Everybody* can jump," Mike told them.

"Yes, but not like me," Freddy said. "And besides, I can talk loud."

"I can talk loud," Ellen said. "Listen to this." And she screamed. "See how loud I can talk."

"That's enough, Ellen," Mom said.

Dad said, "Freddy, I think it's wonderful that you got the part in the play."

Mom kissed him and said, "We're all proud of you, Freddy."

Ellen laughed. "Green Kangaroo, Green Kangaroo," she said over and over again.

Mike just shook his head and said, "I still can't believe it. *He's* going to be the Green Kangaroo."

"It's true," Freddy said. "Just me. All by myself – the only Green Kangaroo in the play."

The next two weeks were busy ones for Freddy. He had to practice being the Green Kangaroo a lot. He practiced at school on the stage. He practiced at home, too. He made kangaroo faces in front of the mirror. He did kangaroo jumps on his bed. He even dreamed about Green Kangaroos at night.

Finally, the day of the play came. The whole family would be there. Some of their neighbors were coming too.

Mom hugged Freddy extra hard as he left for school. "We'll be there watching you, Green Kangaroo," she said.

After lunch Ms. Gumber called to Freddy. "Time to go now. Time to get into your costume." Ms. Gumber walked to the hall with Freddy.

Then she whispered, "We'll be in the second row. Break a leg."

"Break a leg?" Freddy said.

Ms. Gumber laughed. "That means good luck when you're in a play."

"Oh," Freddy said. "I thought you meant I should fall off the stage and *really* break a leg."

Ms. Gumber laughed again. She ruffled Freddy's hair.

Freddy went to Ms. Matson's room. The girls in the sixth grade had made his costume. They all giggled when Ms. Matson helped Freddy into it. His Green Kangaroo suit covered all of him. It even had green feet. Only his face stuck out. Ms. Matson put some green dots on it. "We'll wash them off later. Okay?"

"Okay," Freddy mumbled. He
jumped over to the mirror. He looked at
himself. He really felt like a Green Kangaroo.

It was time for the play to begin.
Freddy waited backstage with the fifth
and sixth graders who were in the play.
They looked at him and smiled. He tried
to smile back. But the smile wouldn't
come. His heart started to beat faster. His
stomach bounced up and down. He felt
funny. Then Ms. Matson leaned close to
him. She said, "They're waiting for you,
Freddy. Go ahead."

He jumped out onto the stage. He looked out into the audience. All those people were down there – somewhere. He knew they were. It was very quiet. He could hear his heart. He thought he saw Mom and Dad. He thought he saw Ellen. He thought he saw Mike and Ms. Gumber and his second grade class and all of his neighbors, too. They were all out there somewhere. They were all in the middle of the audience. But Freddy wasn't in the middle. He was all by himself up on the stage. He had a job to do. He *had* to be the Green Kangaroo.

Freddy smiled. His heart slowed down. His stomach stayed still. He felt better. He smiled a bigger, wider smile. He felt good.

"HELLO EVERYONE," Freddy said. "I AM THE GREEN KANGAROO. WELCOME."

The play began. Freddy did his big and little jumps. Every few minutes one of the fifth or sixth graders in the play said to him, "And who are you?"

Freddy jumped around and answered. "Me? I am the Green Kangaroo!" It was easy. That was all he had to say. It was fun, too. Every time he said it the audience laughed. Freddy liked it when they laughed. It was a funny play.

When it was all over everyone on the stage took a bow. Then Ms. Matson came out and waited for the audience to get quiet. She said, "A special thank you to our second grader, Freddy Dissel. He played the part of the Green Kangaroo."

Freddy jumped over to the middle of the stage. He took a big, low bow all by himself. The audience clapped hard for a long time.

Freddy didn't care much about wearing Mike's clothes any more. He didn't care much about sharing Mike's room either. He didn't care much that Ellen was small and cute. He didn't even care much about being the one in the middle. He felt just great being Freddy Dissel.

Freckle Juice

ISBN: 0-440-42813-0

Nicky has freckles.

They cover his face, his ears, and the whole back of his neck. If Andrew had freckles like Nicky, his mother would never know if his neck was dirty. But how exactly do you *get* freckles?

For fifty cents, know-it-all Sharon has the answer—a secret family freckle recipe. Fifty cents is a lot of money, but Andrew is desperate.

It's not until after he goes home and carefully mixes the strange combination of ingredients that he realizes he might be getting more than he paid for.

FROM BESTSELLING AUTHOR
Judy Blume
ILLUSTRATED BY James Stevenson

GREAT Relations—**PAIN**fully Funny!

Hilarious chapter books that showcase
the joys, the fun, and the frustrations
of being someone's sibling!

www.painandthegreatone.com

Delacorte
Press